*The Boxcar Children Mysteries*

The Boxcar Children
Surprise Island
The Yellow House Mystery
Mystery Ranch
Mike's Mystery
Blue Bay Mystery
The Woodshed Mystery
The Lighthouse Mystery
Mountain Top Mystery
Schoolhouse Mystery
Caboose Mystery
Houseboat Mystery
Snowbound Mystery
Tree House Mystery
Bicycle Mystery
Mystery in the Sand
Mystery Behind the Wall
Bus Station Mystery
Benny Uncovers a Mystery
The Haunted Cabin Mystery
The Deserted Library Mystery
The Animal Shelter Mystery
The Old Motel Mystery
The Mystery of the Hidden Painting
The Amusement Park Mystery
The Mystery of the Mixed-Up Zoo
The Camp-Out Mystery
The Mystery Girl
The Mystery Cruise
The Disappearing Friend Mystery
The Mystery of the Singing Ghost
Mystery in the Snow
The Pizza Mystery
The Mystery Horse
The Mystery at the Dog Show
The Castle Mystery
The Mystery of the Lost Village
The Mystery on the Ice
The Mystery of the Purple Pool
The Ghost Ship Mystery
The Mystery in Washington, DC
The Canoe Trip Mystery
The Mystery of the Hidden Beach
The Mystery of the Missing Cat
The Mystery at Snowflake Inn
The Mystery on Stage
The Dinosaur Mystery
The Mystery of the Stolen Music
The Mystery at the Ball Park
The Chocolate Sundae Mystery
The Mystery of the Hot Air Balloon
The Mystery Bookstore
The Pilgrim Village Mystery
The Mystery of the Stolen Boxcar
The Mystery in the Cave
The Mystery on the Train
The Mystery at the Fair
The Mystery of the Lost Mine
The Guide Dog Mystery
The Hurricane Mystery
The Pet Shop Mystery
The Mystery of the Secret Message
The Firehouse Mystery
The Mystery in San Francisco
The Niagara Falls Mystery
The Mystery at the Alamo
The Outer Space Mystery
The Soccer Mystery
The Mystery in the Old Attic
The Growling Bear Mystery
The Mystery of the Lake Monster
The Mystery at Peacock Hall
The Windy City Mystery
The Black Pearl Mystery
The Cereal Box Mystery
The Panther Mystery
The Mystery of the Queen's Jewels
The Stolen Sword Mystery
The Basketball Mystery

The Movie Star Mystery
The Mystery of the Pirate's Map
The Ghost Town Mystery
The Mystery of the Black Raven
The Mystery in the Mall
The Mystery in New York
The Gymnastics Mystery
The Poison Frog Mystery
The Mystery of the Empty Safe
The Home Run Mystery
The Great Bicycle Race Mystery
The Mystery of the Wild Ponies
The Mystery in the Computer Game
The Mystery at the Crooked House
The Hockey Mystery
The Mystery of the Midnight Dog
The Mystery of the Screech Owl
The Summer Camp Mystery
The Copycat Mystery
The Haunted Clock Tower Mystery
The Mystery of the Tiger's Eye
The Disappearing Staircase Mystery
The Mystery on Blizzard Mountain
The Mystery of the Spider's Clue
The Candy Factory Mystery
The Mystery of the Mummy's Curse
The Mystery of the Star Ruby
The Stuffed Bear Mystery
The Mystery of Alligator Swamp
The Mystery at Skeleton Point
The Tattletale Mystery
The Comic Book Mystery
The Great Shark Mystery
The Ice Cream Mystery
The Midnight Mystery
The Mystery in the Fortune Cookie
The Black Widow Spider Mystery
The Radio Mystery
The Mystery of the Runaway Ghost
The Finders Keepers Mystery
The Mystery of the Haunted Boxcar
The Clue in the Corn Maze
The Ghost of the Chattering Bones
The Sword of the Silver Knight
The Game Store Mystery
The Mystery of the Orphan Train
The Vanishing Passenger
The Giant Yo-Yo Mystery
The Creature in Ogopogo Lake
The Rock 'n' Roll Mystery
The Secret of the Mask
The Seattle Puzzle
The Ghost in the First Row
The Box That Watch Found
A Horse Named Dragon
The Great Detective Race
The Ghost at the Drive-In Movie
The Mystery of the Traveling Tomatoes
The Spy Game
The Dog-Gone Mystery
The Vampire Mystery
Superstar Watch
The Spy in the Bleachers
The Amazing Mystery Show
The Clue in the Recycling Bin
Monkey Trouble
The Zombie Project
The Great Turkey Heist
The Garden Thief

# THE GARDEN THIEF

created by
GERTRUDE CHANDLER WARNER

Library of Congress Cataloging-in-Publication Data is on file.

ISBN: 978-0-8075-2751-1 (hardcover)
ISBN: 978-0-8075-2752-8 (paperback)

Published in 2012 by Albert Whitman & Company,
250 South Northwest Highway, Suite 320, Park Ridge, Illinois, 60068.

Printed in the United States of America.


10 9 8 7 6 5 4 3 2 1 LB 16 15 14 13 12 11

*Cover illustration by Tim Jessel.*
*Interior illustrations by Robert Dunn.*

For information about Albert Whitman & Company,
visit our web site at www.albertwhitman.com.

## *Contents*

# THE GARDEN THIEF

CHAPTER 1

# *Mr. Yee Has a Problem*

"It's raining," said Benny as he looked out the window. "And somebody is walking funny." Benny was six years old, the youngest of the four Alden children.

Violet, his ten-year-old sister, put down her violin and came to the window. "It's not raining hard," she said. "This is just a drizzle." She looked down the long driveway, at the person walking toward their house. "That man is tilting toward the right as he walks."

Jessie, who had been reading a book, put it down and came to the window. She was twelve years old and sometimes took charge of her younger brother and sister. Jessie looked out the window. "That's Mr. Albert Yee," she said. "Grandfather's friend. And I agree, he is walking funny."

The Alden children lived with their grandfather, James Alden. After their parents died, the children had run away from home and lived in a boxcar in the woods. They thought that their grandfather, whom they had never met, was a very mean person. They didn't want to live with him. But their grandfather found them and they saw he was a good person. Now Benny, Violet, Jessie, and Henry lived with him in a big house in Greenfield, Connecticut.

"Why are you all staring out the window?" asked Henry. At fourteen, he was the oldest. Henry loved tools and he loved to fix things. In fact, he had just come up from the basement, where he had a small workshop. "Hey," he said, "that's Mr. Yee. And he has a broken arm."

"Yes," said Jessie. "Now I can see the cast."

"Poor Mr. Yee," said Violet. "It must hurt. See how he's holding his arm?"

Benny ran to the door to let Mr. Yee in. He reached it at the same time as Mrs. McGregor did. She was the Aldens' housekeeper and a great cook.

Mrs. McGregor opened the door. "Why, hello, Mr. Yee," she said. "Come right in."

"What happened to your arm?" Benny asked.

"Hello, Benny," said Mr. Yee. "I fell and broke it."

The other children came to the door and said hello to Mr. Yee. Mrs. McGregor asked him if he would like some hot tea. He said yes, and soon everybody found themselves sitting at the table in Mrs. McGregor's kitchen.

The cast on Mr. Yee's right arm went all the way from his wrist to the middle of his upper arm. Violet noticed that Mr. Yee couldn't seem to sit comfortably at the table. And he had to hold his teacup in his left hand.

"How did you break your arm?" Jessie asked him.

"Stupid accident," Mr. Yee said angrily. "Stupid. I don't want to talk about it now."

The Aldens looked at each other. They felt bad for Mr. Yee.

"Now don't you worry," Mrs. McGregor told him. "Your arm will heal and you'll be fine."

Mr. Yee looked at her. "How do you know my arm will heal?" he asked.

"Well," said Mrs. McGregor, "because you're healthy and you eat healthful foods. Think of all the vegetables you grow and eat. You're a wonderful gardener," she said.

Mr. Yee shook his head back and forth. "I cannot tend to my garden this year," he said. "I thought I could, but I can't. Not with my arm in a cast. That's why I'm here. I want to ask James for help."

"Grandfather isn't here," said Henry. "He's visiting his sister, our Aunt Jane, until Friday."

Mr. Yee sighed. "Then it's no use," he said.

"I can't tend the garden without help."

"We can help," said Violet softly. "We love to help."

"Yes," said Jessie. She passed a plate of Mrs. McGregor's freshly baked cookies to Mr. Yee. "We're very good at helping. We'll help you tend your garden."

Mr. Yee sat up a little straighter. "Really?" he asked, looking at each of the children.

"We are quick learners," said Henry.

"And I love vegetables," said Benny. In fact, Benny loved food of all kind.

Mr. Yee sipped his tea and seemed to be thinking. Finally he spoke.

"Each year, prizes are given for the best vegetables grown in the community gardens. I have won blue ribbons three years in a row. Once for my tomatoes, once for my cucumbers, and once for my carrots." He looked at the children. "Maybe, with your help, my garden will produce good vegetables. That is the important thing." He sipped more tea. "And maybe, just maybe, I will win another blue ribbon this year."

"What's a community garden?" Benny asked.

Henry, who had learned it in school, explained that a community garden was a large plot of land on which many different people had gardens.

Mr. Yee nodded. "That is correct," he said. "Instead of each of us having a little garden in our back yards, we all go to the same place to grow our gardens."

"That sounds wonderful," said Violet.

"It is," said Mr. Yee. "Although . . . ."

"Although what?" asked Jessie.

"This year isn't like before," said Mr. Yee. "There have been problems this year."

"What problems?" asked Benny.

"Somebody has been driving an ATV through the gardens, running over plants," said Mr. Yee. He looked at Benny. "An ATV is an All Terrain Vehicle," he said.

Benny nodded. "I know that. An ATV can have three wheels or four wheels. Vroooommmmm!"

Mr. Yee smiled at Benny. "No four-wheeled

ATV is guilty," he said. "Whoever is running over plants drives a three-wheeled ATV."

"That's mean to ride over plants," said Henry, "Do you know who's doing it?"

Mr. Yee shook his head. "And that's not all. Somebody has been stealing vegetables from the gardens. Last week they took all of my young broccoli plants."

"A vandal and a thief," Jessie said.

"Or a vandal who's also a thief," said Henry.

"That's not good," Jessie said as she looked at her brothers and sister. They nodded their heads.

"We will help you with your garden, Mr. Yee," said Jessie. "And we'll also find out who's been harming the gardens."

Mr. Yee looked at the children. "Well," he said, "James always says that the four of you can solve mysteries."

"Oh, they sure can," said Mrs. McGregor as she collected the cups and plates.

Violet looked out the window. "The drizzle has stopped," she said. "Maybe we can go with you to the community garden now," she said to Mr. Yee.

Mrs. McGregor spoke up. "But how did you get here?" she asked Mr. Yee. "You can't drive, not with your arm in that big cast. And you can't ride your bike, either."

"I walked," said Mr. Yee with a frown. "I miss my bike."

"Well," said Mrs. McGregor, taking off her apron, "I'll drive all of you to the gardens, then I'll come back for you later."

Mr. Yee stood. "Thank you so much," he said.

* * *

"Wow!" said Benny as Mrs. McGregor turned into the lane marked Greenfield Community Gardens. "Look at all the plants!"

"The gardens are right across the road from the Kirk Farm," said Jessie. "My class took a tour of the working farm last year."

Mr. Yee started to get out of the car. Violet got out of the back seat and opened the front car door to help him.

"I loved riding my bike here each day," he

said. "Now I must walk, until my arm heals."

After Mrs. McGregor drove off, Mr. Yee told the children he would give them a brief tour of the community gardens before he showed them how to help.

"The gardens are divided into five sections," he told them. "Sections A through E. Each section has five garden plots."

Jessie noticed five tall posts, each marking one of the five sections.

"We'll save Section A for last," explained Mr. Yee as he walked toward Section E. The Aldens followed him.

At Section E, Mr. Yee showed the children five different plots, numbered one through five.

"Everything is so neat," said Henry. "Every section is marked, and every plot is marked."

Jessie agreed. She looked around. "And there are no fences."

Mr. Yee scratched the fingers of his right hand, where they emerged from the cast. "There is one fence," he said. "You'll see it soon."

As Mr. Yee led the children around Sections E, D, C, and B, he said hello to people who were working in their gardens. When he stopped to talk to the people, he introduced each of the children. "Thanks to these kind children," he said, "I can grow vegetables this year."

When they rounded the corner of Section B, the children stopped. In front of them was a very large, very long section marked A.

"This is huge," said Henry. "It's twice as big as any of the other sections."

"Yes," said Mr. Yee, "and each plot is much larger than the plots in Sections B through E."

"Why?" asked Benny.

"Because some people want smaller plots and others want bigger plots." said Mr. Yee. "Many of the gardeners who win prizes garden in Section A."

As he talked, Mr. Yee led them forward.

"Look!" shouted Benny. "Rabbits!" He pointed toward one end of Section A, where two white rabbits with brown and black spots hopped into one of the gardens.

Violet noticed that one of the plots — the one right in the middle of Section A — had a chain link fence all around it.

Henry saw two kids standing in front of one of the plots. One was a girl of about twelve, the other was a boy of maybe seventeen.

Mr. Yee saw the boy and girl. "Trouble," he muttered. "Trouble, trouble." He turned to Jessie, who was walking next to him. "They are standing in front of my plot, Plot Number Two."

"Who are they?" asked Jessie. She noticed that the girl was wearing a cast on her left leg and holding a large green trash bag. The strap-on cast was bright orange.

Before Mr. Yee could answer, the girl walked up to them. "I'm Lucasta Kirk," she said. "I raise prize-winning rabbits. Orange is my favorite color."

Lucasta frowned at Violet, who was wearing a purple shirt. Violet loved all shades of purple, including lavender and violet.

"Purple is my least favorite color," said Lucasta.

Violet's feelings were hurt by Lucasta's remark. She thought that Lucasta did not have good manners.

Henry introduced himself and his sisters and brother.

The other boy said he was Alex Kirk, Lucasta's brother.

"Do you have a plot in the community gardens?" Jessie asked Alex and Lucasta.

"I have plot number five," said Alex. "And Lucasta has plot number four."

Jessie looked at the size of each plot. "That's a lot of land to garden," she said.

"We know how to do it," said Alex. "We grew up on a farm. That's our farm across the street." He pointed to a large white barn and a white farmhouse surrounded by fields.

"I'm not gardening this year," Lucasta said. "I'm spending all my time raising my rabbits, so that they win top prize.

Also," she added, "Mr. Yee ran over me with his bicycle and broke my leg and it's too hard for me to garden with a broken leg."

"That is not true!" shouted Mr. Yee. "I did not run over you with my bicycle! Your rabbits ran right in front of me as I was riding, and when I tried to not run over your rabbits, I flew over my handlebars and broke my arm."

"Your bike hit me and broke my leg!" said Lucasta.

"My bike hit you after I was no longer on it, after I flew over the handlebars and broke my arm because of your rabbits!"

"Please," said Alex, "let's not argue about this again. Lucasta is fine, and I hope that you will be, too, Mr. Yee. You're a very good gardener and I hope you're able to grow wonderful vegetables again this year. Let's forget all about the accident."

"I will never forget," said Lucasta. "If my rabbits don't win first prize at the fair this summer, I will hold Mr. Yee responsible." She turned and limped away.

CHAPTER 2

# *Cool as a Cucumber*

Alex Kirk said he had to take care of his garden and left.

Mr. Yee took several deep breaths, then said, "Come, let's walk through my garden plot."

The Aldens followed him, careful to not step on any plants. That was a bit hard to do because the plants were sprawled out everywhere.

And so were weeds. Jessie knew that the tall grass-like stalks didn't belong in the middle of the plants. Mr. Yee needs our help to weed his garden, she thought. He can't do it with one arm in a cast.

Mr. Yee stopped in the middle of a long path. He pointed to the far end of two rows of carrots. "Notice how the carrots at the far end of each row are bigger than the ones in the middle of the rows," he said. "And the ones where we're standing are the smallest of the carrots."

The Aldens looked and nodded. "You must have planted some carrots earlier than others," said Henry.

"That is right," said Mr. Yee. "I was able to plant seeds, but I can't weed or thin." He frowned. "My rows are not very straight," he said. "That's because of my broken arm."

Benny looked at the rows of carrots. "But I'll bet the carrots taste good, even though the rows aren't straight."

Mr. Yee looked at Benny. "You have already grasped what is important, Benny — that the vegetables taste good."

"But you would also like to win prizes if

you can," said Violet.

"You have also grasped what is important, Violet," said Mr. Yee. He rubbed his hands together — which was not easy to do because his right arm stuck out at an angle because of the cast.

"So," he said. "Here we have rows of lettuce, radishes, and carrots. They need to be thinned, and they need to be weeded."

"What's thinned mean?" asked Violet.

Mr. Yee squatted so that he was closer to the plants. "If we let all of these carrots grow in one spot, none of them will grow large. But if we pull out some of the carrots, the ones we leave in the ground will grow large." Mr. Yee carefully pulled out a few green tops.

"There's a baby carrot at the end of each one!" said Benny.

"And they're purple!" exclaimed Violet. "I love purple carrots!"

"I have a bucket of clean water over there," said Mr. Yee, pointing. "Could you bring it to me?" he asked Henry.

Henry brought the bucket of water and

Mr. Yee rinsed the tiny carrots in water. Then he tore off the green tops and gave two tiny carrots to each of the children.

"Yum!"said Benny. "They're so sweet."

"And so crisp," said Jessie.

"And so purple!" Violet laughed. "Jessie and I can thin the carrots if you show us how," she said to Mr. Yee. "And also the radishes and lettuce."

Mr. Yee smiled. "That will be wonderful." He showed them how to thin the lettuce and radishes. And he gave them a basket to put the thinnings in. "You can take the thinnings home to Mrs. McGregor," he said.

After he was satisfied that Violet and Jessie were doing a good job, Mr. Yee led Henry and Benny to a different part of the garden.

"What are those?" asked Benny, pointing to large leaves that sprawled across the ground.

A sad look passed over Mr. Yee's face. "Those are my beans and my peas," he explained. "They are climbing plants, but I haven't been able to put up poles or trellises for them to climb on."

"I can do that," Henry offered. "Tomorrow I'll bring my toolbox."

Mr. Yee looked happy. "Thank you," he said. "You can use the lumber I have here in the garden, past the strawberries."

"Strawberries?" said Benny. "Where are they?"

"Look down, Benny." Mr. Yee chuckled as he pointed at Benny's feet, where long rows of short plants grew.

"I see leaves," said Benny as he looked down, "but I don't see strawberries."

With difficulty Mr. Lee squatted and gently ran his hand underneath the strawberry plant leaves, lifting them upward.

"Strawberries!" said Benny.

"And they look delicious," said Henry as he studied the bright red fruits.

Mr. Yee plucked a ripe strawberry and handed it to Benny. He plucked another and handed it to Henry.

"This is the best-tasting strawberry I've ever had," said Henry. "Do you win prizes for your strawberries, too, Mr. Yee?"

Mr. Yee struggled to his feet and laughed. "Not yet. But maybe if Benny helps me, we can win this year."

"Really?" asked Benny, who wanted more strawberries. "What should I do?"

"Well," said Mr. Yee, "I have two long rows of strawberries." He pointed to the row they were standing at and the one next to it.

Henry whistled. "Each row is at least twenty-five feet long," he said.

"Thirty feet," corrected Mr. Yee proudly.

"Can you eat that many strawberries all by yourself?" asked Benny as he looked at the two long rows. Benny thought that even he couldn't eat that many berries, no matter how much he loved them.

"No," Mr. Yee answered. "I freeze some and I make strawberry jam from some. But mostly I eat them myself and give them to friends. Lots of friends."

Mr. Yee then explained to Benny that strawberry plants had to be watered before the ground became totally dry. He showed both

Benny and Henry where the water spigots were, one spigot outside each section, and he showed them where he kept his buckets and watering cans.

Henry looked at the water spigot, which was on a pipe that came up from the ground. "Do all community gardens have a water supply?" he asked.

"No," said Mr. Yee. "Many depend on the rainfall, and sometimes on water that people bring in trucks. But Mr. Kirk had an irrigation system in this field, and after he loaned the field to the town of Greenfield, the town paid to install the upright pipes and spigots."

"It's wonderful of Mr. Kirk to loan his land for a community garden," Henry said.

Mr. Yee agreed.

"Now let me show you my tomato plants," he said. "Last year I won a blue ribbon for my tomatoes."

Henry and Benny followed Mr. Yee back into the garden, past the peas and beans, past the strawberry plants, and around a corner.

As they rounded the corner, Mr. Yee cried out, "No! No! What has happened? Somebody has broken my tomato stakes!"

Indeed, Mr. Yee had a long row of tomato plants, each tied to a strong wooden stake that had been pounded into the ground. But Henry could see that somebody had come along and whacked each stake near the bottom, cracking it. Now the weight of the tomato plants was pulling the stakes outward. Soon the stakes would crack and topple over. And so would the tomato plants.

"Who would do such a terrible thing?" asked Henry.

"The vandal!" shouted Mr. Yee. "The vandal who is trying to destroy the community gardens!" He paced back and forth and ran his hand over his gray hair. "What am I going to do?" he cried. "What am I going to do? My tomato plants are ruined!"

Suddenly a man stood up in the next garden. Henry hadn't seen him before. He must have been kneeling down, weeding, thought Henry.

The man rushed over to Mr. Yee.

"Albert, what's wrong?" asked the man.

Mr. Yee just shook his head sadly and pointed at his tomato plants.

"Oh, no," said the man. "This is terrible." He looked at the plants, then looked at Mr. Yee. "It's the vandal again," he said. "The same person who's been riding his ATV through the gardens."

"Yes," said Mr. Yee.

"Hi," said the man to Henry and Benny. "I'm Roger Walski. You can call me Roger.

That's my garden plot." He pointed to plot number one, right next to Mr. Yee's plot number two.

"I'm Henry Alden," said Henry. "And this is my brother Benny. Our sisters Jessie and Violet are here, too, over by the carrots and lettuce."

Roger Walski nodded. "I'm sorry this happened to your plants, Albert. But I've been telling you, this isn't a good site for the community gardens. We should move further down the road, to new land."

Mr. Yee shook his head back and forth. "No, Roger, I disagree. We Chinese believe in luck, and this is just bad luck. It will go away. This is a wonderful spot to garden."

"You'll have to give up on your tomatoes," said Mr. Walski. "With your broken arm, you won't be able to replace these stakes."

"I'll replace the stakes," said Henry. "Mr. Yee will show me how to take out the broken ones without hurting the plants."

Mr. Yee looked at Henry gratefully. "Thank you, Henry. We can do that tomorrow."

Roger Walski frowned. "Well," he said, "I'm glad you can save your tomatoes. But you won't win first prize for them this year, not with this setback."

"I suppose you think you will win a blue ribbon with your cucumbers," snapped Mr. Yee, who did not like the thought of losing.

"Yes, I will," said Mr. Walski with a smile.

"I love cucumbers," said Benny.

Mr. Walski looked at Henry and Benny. "Come with me," he said, "and I'll teach you something about cucumbers."

"First we have to help Mr. Yee," said Henry.

"No, no," said Mr. Yee. "Let us go see Roger's cucumbers."

The four of them walked down a path between rows of plants that Henry didn't recognize. They stepped across a string marker that separated Mr. Yee's garden plot from Roger's, and Roger led them down a path to a row of trellises shaped like teepees.

Henry liked the way that three poles were pushed into the ground at an angle, tilted toward each other, and tied at the top. "Did you build these?" he asked.

"Yes," said Roger.

"They're very well built," said Henry. "And they seem to work so well."

"They do work well," said Roger. "The cucumber vines climb up the poles and hang from them. That means they don't spread on the ground, and that means I have more ground space to grow other vegetables."

Benny leaned over backward and tried to look up into the teepee-shaped structure.

Roger Walski laughed. "Here," he said, pushing aside some leaves and revealing a cucumber.

"Wow!" said Benny. "Are they ready to eat yet?"

"Some will be ready to eat tomorrow," said Roger. "And others will be ready in two weeks. And I'll have more cucumbers that will be ready for the Greenfield Fair."

Mr. Yee smashed a clump of dirt with the toe of his shoe. "You were going to tell Henry and Benny something about cucumbers," he reminded Roger. "I hope it wasn't just bragging that you will win a blue ribbon."

Roger looked at the children. "Here's what I wanted to teach you: the inside of a cucumber is always cooler than the temperature around it. That's why people say 'cool as a cucumber' — because the cucumber is cool on the inside."

"What does that mean?" asked Benny.

"To be cool as a cucumber is to be calm," said Henry. "It means you don't get angry or flustered."

"That's right," said Roger. "And I am cool. As cool as a cucumber."

"What do you mean?" asked Henry.

Roger stood straight. "It means that despite the vandalism and despite the fact that somebody might be stealing vegetables, I remain calm."

Mr. Yee shook his head at this. "It is easy to remain calm," he said, "when it is not *your* garden that has been harmed."

"I remain calm," Roger repeated, "because I'm the one who knows what must be done."

Everybody looked at Roger Walski.

"What must be done?" asked Henry.

"We community gardeners must move to a new location," said Roger.

Just as Roger was speaking, a young woman rode up on a racing bike, dismounted, and walked toward the middle plot — the plot that had a fence all around it.

"That's Taylor Harris," said Roger. He scowled. "She claims her vegetables will win first prize. But she doesn't want any of us to see them. That's why she built a fence all around her garden. Not a very friendly thing to do."

CHAPTER 3

# *Why a Fence?*

Jessie and Violet, who were still thinning and weeding plants, saw a young woman ride her bike almost right up to them.

"Hi," she said as she locked her bike to the chain link fence that surrounded plot number three. "I'm Taylor Harris."

Jessie stood up and introduced herself and Violet. They shook hands with Taylor Harris, who was dressed in purple and yellow cycling gear. Violet thought the colors looked really good against Taylor's black skin.

"Are you helping Mr. Yee?" Taylor asked as she took a pair of dumbbells from her bike pack. Taylor began to do arm exercises with the dumbbells.

"Yes, we're helping Mr. Yee. This is our first day. Are you training for a contest?" Jessie asked.

"No, no," said Taylor. "I just like to keep fit."

Jessie and Violet watched as Taylor put the dumbbells back into her cycle pack. She pulled out something else that looked heavy.

"Oops," said Taylor, looking down at the ground. "Where did it go?"

"What did you lose?" asked Violet, who thought she saw something fall.

"A one-pound piece of metal, like a slug. It goes inside a slot in this leg weight, so I can make them lighter or heavier." She held out a leg weight so that Jessie and Violet could see it.

"It has five little pockets sewn in," said Violet.

Taylor nodded, still looking around. "I can fit one- or two-pound weights into each slot."

Jessie spied the dark weight on the ground. It was hard to see because it blended in with the color of the dirt. Jessie bent and picked it up. "Here it is," she said, handing it to Taylor.

"Thank you," said Taylor. She looked at Jessie and Violet, then she looked down at the thinning and weeding they had done.

"Hmmmm," she said, "you girls are doing a very good job."

"Thanks," said Jessie and Violet together.

"Mr. Yee would like to win more blue ribbons," said Taylor, "but he won't. This year, it's my turn to win, and I'll do whatever I need to do to win those blue ribbons."

Jessie thought Taylor Harris looked very determined as she said this.

"In fact," continued Taylor, "I'd better do my leg exercises later. Time for me to garden."

"What vegetables do you grow?" asked Violet.

"Oh, you name it, I grow it," said Taylor. "But kale is my favorite. I love its color, its crinkly leaves, and its taste. I eat it raw or cooked, hot or cold."

"Which vegetables do you hope to win blue ribbons for?" Jessie asked. "Just kale?"

"All of them," said Taylor. "I've never won a blue ribbon before and I'm tired of not winning. This year I'm growing the best vegetables ever!"

Jessie and Violet watched as Taylor took a

key out of her racing shorts and put it into the heavy lock on the garden gate.

"I built this fence and gate last month, all by myself," she told them, "to protect my vegetables."

"From rabbits?" asked Violet, who remembered that there had been rabbits hopping around the gardens earlier. They were probably Lucasta's rabbits, but Violet wasn't sure.

Taylor frowned. "No," she replied. "I want to protect my vegetables from two-legged thieves."

"Oh," said Violet, "Mr. Yee told us somebody was stealing vegetables. What a mean thing to do, to steal the food somebody else has grown."

Taylor pressed her lips tight and nodded. She seemed angry just thinking about it. "This is the first year we've had a thief," she said. "Last year and the year before, everything was fine. But this year — this year somebody has been stealing vegetables almost every day! That's why I built my fence."

"Somebody is stealing vegetables every single day?" asked Jessie.

Taylor Harris nodded. "Just about every day."

"From every plot in the community gardens?" Jessie asked.

Taylor stopped to think. "Mostly Section A," she said, "though some people in B and C have had vegetables stolen, too."

"That's strange," said Violet.

"Maybe," said Taylor.

"Our brothers are also helping Mr. Yee," Jessie told Taylor. "And the four of us are going to find out who is vandalizing the gardens and who's stealing vegetables."

Taylor looked at Violet and Jessie. "Well," she said at last, "good luck." Then she stepped into her garden and closed the gate behind herself.

Jessie and Violet stretched and brushed off their knees. "Mrs. McGregor will be picking us up soon," said Jessie. "We can give her the thinnings for salad."

"I like Taylor," said Violet. "She looks good

in purple and yellow."

Just as Jessie stooped down to pick up the basket of thinned lettuce, radishes, and carrots, they heard Taylor Harris shouting loudly.

"My lettuce is gone!" she shouted. "And my kale! My lettuce and kale are gone!"

Jessie and Violet opened the gate to Taylor's garden and rushed in. And Henry, Benny, Mr. Yee, and another man came running in after them.

CHAPTER 4

# *Rabbits Everywhere*

"Lucasta's rabbits did this!" shouted Taylor. "I know they did! Her rabbits ate all my lettuce and kale!"

Henry looked down at the ground, where the lettuce and kale had been. He saw small holes where the plants had been. "I don't think it was rabbits," said Henry.

"Who are you?" Taylor demanded.

Henry explained who he and Benny were, and then Roger Walski told Jessie and Violet who he was. After everybody seemed to know who everybody else was, Taylor said, "It was those rabbits, I know it was. I won't stand for this!"

Henry shook his head. "If rabbits ate your plants, there would be some leaves left. We would see teeth marks on the leaves, where the rabbits nibbled them. But there's nothing left of your lettuce or kale." Henry pointed to the holes in the ground. "Not even the roots are left. Your plants were pulled out of the ground."

"Henry is right," said Mr. Yee to Taylor.

"I don't care what Henry says," shouted Taylor. "There are rabbits everywhere, dozens of rabbits! Big gray ones! White ones with spots all over! I just know the rabbits did it."

Roger spoke up. "Whoever did this, it just goes to show that this is a bad spot for a community garden. There's good land that's empty a mile up the road. We can all get together and have the village of Greenfield sign a lease for that land. We can garden in a better place next year. No vandals," he said, "no thieves."

Taylor Harris was so angry that she wasn't really listening to Roger. "I'm going to march right up that hill," she said, pointing toward the Kirk farm across the dirt road, "and into that barn. That's where the rabbits are. They just hippity-hop down here and eat whatever they like."

Taylor stomped out of her garden and up the hill. Everybody else followed her.

"But Taylor," said Jessie, trying to keep up with the angry young woman, "how could the rabbits get into your garden? They couldn't open the gate."

"They probably dug under the fence," said Taylor as she strode uphill.

"But you didn't look to see if that was true," said Jessie. "And besides, like Henry said, the rabbits wouldn't pull your plants out by the roots."

"I don't trust Lucasta," said Taylor. "She probably dropped the rabbits over my fence and let them eat everything."

"But how would the rabbits get out?"

asked Henry.

"Don't argue with me," Taylor said. "The rabbits are responsible."

By this time Taylor, the Aldens, Mr. Yee and Roger had all crossed the dirt road and were walking toward an old white barn whose wide doors were open.

Taylor was about to walk through the open doors when Alex Kirk stepped out right in front of her.

"Have you come to see my father?" he asked.

"No," said Taylor.

Lucasta came up right behind Alex. "Have you come to see my rabbits?" she asked.

Benny looked past Alex and Lucasta and into the barn. "Look at all the rabbits!" he said.

"Prize-winning rabbits," said Lucasta.

"Sneaky, lettuce-eating rabbits," said Taylor. "Rabbits who got into my garden and ate all my lettuce and kale!"

"When?" asked Alex.

Taylor looked puzzled. "Well, I don't know

when, exactly. Some time between last night and this morning."

"Lucasta's rabbits have been in their cages all that time. They haven't been out."

"Not true," said Mr. Yee, shaking his head. "There were two rabbits out this morning. We saw them when we saw you."

Alex and Lucasta looked at each other and didn't say anything.

"The rabbits were white and they had big brown spots and big black spots," said Benny. "Like a pinto pony."

"That's just two rabbits," said Alex. "They were the only ones out, weren't they, Lucasta?"

"Yes," said Lucasta. "Only Petra and Petrino were out. None of the other rabbits were out."

"Your leg!" exclaimed Mr. Yee suddenly, pointing at Lucasta's left leg. "You are not wearing your cast. Has your leg healed already?"

"No," said Lucasta angrily. "I was just giving it a rest from the cast. I wasn't walking around much."

Violet watched as Lucasta limped over to a nearby bench and grabbed her bright orange walking cast and strapped it onto her left leg.

"There!" Lucasta said to Mr. Yee. "Are you satisfied?"

Mr. Yee just scowled without saying anything.

"I wish you wouldn't wear that cast," Alex told his sister. "Your leg is healed, you don't need that cast."

"Young bones heal quicker than old bones," muttered Mr. Yee.

"I need the cast," said Lucasta.

"I don't care about your cast!" shouted Taylor. "And I don't care what you say about your rabbits being locked up! Somehow or other, your rabbits are responsible for eating my lettuce and kale. I expected to win blue ribbons for my lettuce and especially for my kale, and now I have to start all over again."

"My rabbits didn't eat your lettuce and kale," Lucasta told Taylor. "Their cages are locked from the outside, so they can't escape."

"So," said Mr. Yee, "did you let your rabbits out on purpose, so they ran in front of my bike and made me fall and break my arm?"

"That was an accident," said Lucasta. "I forgot to lock the cages."

"Well, maybe this time was an accident, too," said Taylor. "I would like to see the cages."

"I have nothing to hide," said Lucasta. "Everybody can look."

The small crowd followed Lucasta as she led the way to the back of the barn.

Henry noticed many rabbit hutches, as many as thirty. Each one had a beautiful rabbit inside. Off in one corner, he noticed an ATV. It had three wheels.

Benny went right up to one of the lower hutches and put his face against the wire. The rabbit that was inside the cage pressed its nose against the wire.

Benny laughed. "That tickles!" he said, rubbing his nose.

Lucasta twisted the wooden handle that locked the rabbit hutch from the outside.

She opened the door and gently lifted the spotted rabbit into her arms and stroked it.

The rabbit looked at Benny. The rabbit's nose twitched.

"It has a pink nose," said Benny. "And the rabbit in the next cage has a black nose."

"There are many different kinds of rabbits," Lucasta explained, "but I raise only Rex and American rabbits. This is a Rex."

She returned the Rex rabbit to its hutch,

closed the lock, and moved to the next cage, which had a gray rabbit inside. Again she opened the hutch and removed the rabbit. "This is an American blue," she said, stroking the rabbit. "Its fur is so gray and black that the rabbit looks blue."

"Your rabbits are beautiful," said Violet, who admired the rabbits' glossy fur and cute noses and long ears.

"All of my rabbits are prize-winning rabbits," said Lucasta. "I give them the best food and the best care."

"Do you feed them a special food to keep them so healthy?" asked Jessie.

"I feed them special rabbit food that we buy at the farmers store," Lucasta answered. "And I feed them the best and freshest vegetables like cucumbers, broccoli, lettuce, chard, carrots, beans, and peas."

"Wow," said Benny. "Rabbits like a lot of different foods."

Jessie noticed an apron hanging from the end of the cages. The apron had many pockets, and a carrot was sticking out of one of the pockets. There was a large green trash bag next to the apron.

"Is that where you keep the vegetables?" she asked, pointing to the apron.

Lucasta frowned.

"No," said Alex as he pulled the apron and trash bag from the wall and rolled them up. He put them on top of the rabbit cages. "That's just an old cobbler's apron."

Alex handed the carrot that had been in the apron to Lucasta and she fed it to the rabbit she was holding.

"I used to feed my rabbits all the vegetables I grew," she said, "but when Mr. Yee broke my leg, I couldn't garden this year."

"I did not break your leg!" shouted Mr. Yee. "Your rabbits ran in front of my bicycle and made me break my arm!"

"I can grow all the vegetables Lucasta needs," said Alex.

"I deserve all of my blue ribbons," said Lucasta.

Taylor Harris sighed. "I deserve blue ribbons, too. I'm going back to my garden, and I better never see one of your rabbits inside it," she said.

Taylor left.

"This is too bad," said Roger Walski.

Henry looked at him in surprise. The entire time they had been in the barn, Roger hadn't said anything.

"It just goes to show that we should move the community gardens some place else.

Away from vandals, away from thieves, and even away from these prize-winning rabbits."

Roger followed Taylor out the wide barn doors. "My cucumbers need my attention," he said as he left.

"We are leaving, also," said Mr. Yee. "I don't like rabbits."

The Aldens followed him out the door.

As the five of them walked back to Mr. Yee's plot, they talked.

"I like the rabbits," said Benny.

"Me, too," said Violet. "And they didn't eat Taylor's lettuce and kale, because rabbits can't open garden gates."

"And rabbits don't pull plants out of the ground," said Henry. "Instead, they nibble the leaves."

The Aldens looked at one another. Something strange was definitely happening at the community garden.

CHAPTER 5

# *Bags of Lettuce and Kale*

Early the next morning Mrs. McGregor handed each of the children a thermal lunch bag.

"There are scrambled egg sandwiches for each of you," she said. "Plus a can of juice and an orange."

Just then Mr. Yee knocked on the back door.

"Is everybody ready?" he asked.

"We're ready," said Henry, stifling a yawn.

"Here is a lunch bag for you, Mr. Yee,"

said Mrs. McGregor. "Scrambled egg sandwiches."

"Thank you," said Mr. Yee. "You are most generous. I will be sure to repay you with excellent vegetables."

Mrs. McGregor drove them all to the community gardens. Henry and Jessie talked to Mr. Yee, but Violet and Benny closed their eyes and fell asleep. When Mrs. McGregor stopped the car at the community gardens, Violet and Benny woke up.

"Are we there?" Benny asked.

"Yes," said Mr. Yee. "We will eat our breakfasts first, then we will tend to the garden."

Mrs. McGregor drove away and the children walked the short distance to the community gardens. They waved to other gardeners in Sections D and E, and also Sections B and C.

When they reached Section A, they saw Taylor's bike chained to her garden fence. Taylor was standing beside the bike. The gate to her garden was open. Henry thought that Taylor looked confused.

"Is anything wrong?" Henry asked as they walked up to her.

"I don't know," answered Taylor. "Can I show you something?"

Henry said yes, and Taylor led everybody into her garden. They followed her down a few rows. Taylor stopped and pointed to two large burlap bags sitting on the ground, right next to the spot where the lettuce and kale had been growing.

"Those were here when I arrived a few minutes ago," said Taylor.

Benny yawned. "What's inside them?" he asked.

"Open them," she said, "and you'll see."

Jessie opened one of the sacks. "Lettuce!" she said. "Lots of lettuce!"

Violet opened the other sack. "Kale," she said. "The whole sack is full of kale."

"What does this mean?" asked Mr. Yee.

"That's what I'd like to know," said Taylor. She looked at the Aldens. "What do you think?" she asked.

Henry spoke first. "I think somebody is trying to make amends," he said.

"I agree," said Jessie. "Somebody is trying to say they're sorry they stole your lettuce and kale yesterday."

"Yes," said Taylor, "I think somebody feels bad about what happened and is giving me this lettuce and kale." She frowned. "It doesn't make sense, though."

"I know what you mean," said Henry. "If somebody stole your lettuce and kale, why would he or she bother giving you more lettuce and kale?"

"But if Lucasta's rabbits ate my lettuce and kale, that makes sense," said Taylor. "Rabbits can't return what they ate, but Lucasta could."

Violet was starting to wake up. Thinking about a mystery always made her feel more alert. "Maybe it's not the same person," she said. "Maybe one person stole the lettuce and kale, but another person is giving you lettuce and kale."

"Hmmm," said Taylor.

"You will have to eat this lettuce and kale very soon," Mr. Yee observed. "Vegetables taste best right after they're picked."

"I can't eat all of this by myself," said Taylor. "Please take as much as you want for yourselves, and I'll donate the rest to the food center."

"We can sprinkle the burlap bags with water," said Mr. Yee, "and put them in the shade, so they stay cool."

Taylor nodded. "I'll do that before I start to weed," she said. "Be sure to take some of these with you when you go home."

"Will you eat some of the lettuce and kale yourself?" Violet asked.

Taylor shook her head.

"Why not?" asked Benny. "I'll bet they taste good."

"They probably do." Taylor laughed. "But these aren't the same kind of lettuce and kale that I grow," she said.

She reached into one bag and pulled out a head of lettuce. "This is a light green butter lettuce," she said, holding it our for the children to see. "It's very tasty, but I was growing a red-tipped leaf lettuce. I like the taste of it better, and I like the dark green color."

Taylor put the lettuce back into one burlap bag and reached into the other bag. She pulled out some kale leaves. "This is a plain green kale," she said, showing the leaves to the children. "I grow a very dark curly kale."

Mr. Yee nodded his head. "These are

good vegetables," he said, "but not as tasty as the kind you grow. If it was the thief who returned these vegetables, I wonder why he didn't return the same kind he took?"

Henry scratched his head. "If the thief returned the exact same kind of vegetables he or she stole, then why steal them in the first place?"

"Do you think this lettuce and kale came from the community gardens?" Jessie asked.

Taylor shrugged her shoulders. "Who knows," she said. "Lots of people here grow butter lettuce and plan kale. Alex grows butter lettuce and plain kale. So does Roger. Lucasta used to grow dark green lettuce and dark curly kale, just like Mr. Yee and I do. But Alex and Lucasta don't enter their vegetables in contests."

"Are you talking about me and my sister?" asked Alex Kirk.

Everybody turned around at the sound of Alex's voice. They saw him at the side of Taylor's garden. He was standing in Lucasta's empty plot, looking at them.

"Yes," said Taylor. "I was saying that you and Lucasta don't enter your vegetables in contests to win blue ribbons."

"That's right," said Alex. "Vegetables are meant to feed people, not to win blue ribbons."

"They can do both things," said Mr. Yee. "They can win blue ribbons, and then they can be eaten."

Alex ignored what Mr. Yee said. "I'm looking for Roger Walski," he said, "but he's not here yet. When you see him, can you give him a message?" he asked.

"Sure," said Henry. "If Mr. Walski is here today, we'll give him a message."

"Good," said Alex. "Please tell him my father still says no."

What did that mean? Jessie wondered.

* * *

The Aldens and Mr. Yee sat on the grass outside the plots and ate their breakfasts. Mr. Yee stopped in his garden first and picked some fresh snow peas and a few strawberries.

They ate the snow peas with their scrambled egg sandwiches and the strawberries after.

"This is a delicious breakfast," said Violet.

"It sure is," said Henry.

"It's the best breakfast I've ever had!" shouted Benny.

The others laughed. "Oh, Benny, you'll say the same thing tomorrow," kidded Jessie.

Benny nodded. "I will if tomorrow is the best breakfast I ever had. And it will be," he added, "if I have some of Mr. Yee's snowpod peas and strawberries!"

"Ah, Benny," said Mr. Yee, "I think you are going to be a good gardener — as long as you don't eat up everything you see!"

They all laughed at that. Then they gathered up their sandwich wrappings and napkins and went to work in the garden.

Henry spent the whole morning building trellises for the peas and beans. He enjoyed the work, and knew that the peas and beans would grow better once they had the trellises for support.

Mr. Yee sat on the ground with Jessie and

Violet and showed them how to transplant young broccoli plants.

"My broccoli plants were stolen last week," he told them. "It is too late to grow broccoli that will win a blue ribbon, but I can still grow some to eat."

"Why is it too late?" asked Violet.

"Because broccoli grows best in cooler weather," he said.

After Mr. Yee was satisfied that Violet and Jessie were doing a good job, and that Henry didn't need his help, he went to check on Benny, who was watering the strawberry plants.

"Ah," said Mr. Yee, "you are doing a very good job, Benny."

"Good," said Benny. "I want the strawberries to be delicious."

Just then they heard the roar of a motor.

Roger Walski zoomed up on a three-wheeled ATV that had a box strapped to the back. He turned off the motor and dismounted.

"Today's the day," he told Benny. "Ready

to taste a garden-fresh cucumber?"

"Yes," said Benny. "I love cucumbers." He turned to Mr. Yee. "May I go taste Mr. Walski's fresh cucumbers?" he asked.

"Of course," said Mr. Yee, "and I will come with you."

Benny and Mr. Yee followed Roger through the maze of garden paths.

But when they reached the place where Roger's cucumbers grew on trellises — the hanging vines were empty!

"My cucumbers!" Roger screamed. "They're all gone! I've been robbed!"

Before Mr. Yee or Benny could say anything, Roger hopped onto his three-wheeled vehicle and roared away, still shouting.

"Poor Roger," said Mr. Yee. "Another victim of this terrible, terrible garden thief."

"Poor Mr. Walski," said Benny. "He's very upset. He isn't as cool as a cucumber."

CHAPTER 6

# *The Lumpy Shapes*

The following morning the children had breakfast at their usual time, in their usual place: at home.

Mrs. McGregor had made granola and served it with milk and fresh strawberries that Benny had brought home from Mr. Yee's garden.

"These are delicious strawberries," said Mrs. McGregor.

"Mr. Yee has two long rows of them," said Benny, "and it's my job to water them. He let me pick these yesterday."

"I'm so glad you're helping Mr. Yee," said Mrs. McGregor. "When your grandfather comes home this afternoon, he'll be very pleased that you're helping his old friend."

"What are we going to do today, Jessie?" Violet asked her sister.

"We're going to harvest carrots and radishes," Jessie answered. "Mr. Yee says we can bring some home to Mrs. McGregor."

Mrs. McGregor was making toast for everybody. She looked confused. "How can you harvest full-grown carrots if they were baby carrots just two days ago?" she asked.

"Because Mr. Yee has spread his plantings two weeks apart," Jessie explained. "He plants a section of carrots every two weeks, and a section of radishes, and lettuce, and kale."

"I see," said Mrs. McGregor. "That way, not all of the vegetables are ready at the same time."

"There's something ready all season long," said Henry. "Except for plants like tomatoes, which Mr. Yee put in all at the same time."

"Are you going to work on the broken towers today?" Jessie asked her brother.

"Yes," said Henry.

"Who would do something mean like break tomato towers?" asked Violet. "Why would they do that?"

"The vandal must have a reason," said Henry.

"What about the thief?" asked Jessie. "I don't think the thief and the vandal are the same person."

Her brothers and sister agreed with her.

The Aldens were still speculating about who might be the vandal and who might be the thief when Mr. Yee arrived. It was time to leave.

As before, Mrs. McGregor drove them all to the community gardens and dropped them off at the end, by Sections D and E. And as before, the children and Mr. Yee walked toward Section A, greeting all the gardeners they passed.

This morning, they did not see Taylor Harris standing at her garden gate, looking perplexed. This morning, they saw two lumpy shapes on the ground, in front of Section A, Plot 1. One shape was long and low. The other shape was round and high.

"What in the world is that?" asked Mr. Yee, scratching underneath the cast of his broken arm. "It's in front of Roger's plot."

"Look!" Benny pointed at something that sat between the two shapes. "It's a Rex rabbit!"

As the Aldens and Mr. Yee got closer, they saw that the long low shape was a sleeping bag, with somebody inside it. The high round shape was a burlap bag. The Rex rabbit was sitting and scratching an ear with a hind leg.

Just then, Lucasta Kirk came around the far corner of Plot 1. She hobbled along slowly, dragging her broken leg, which was covered from toe to knee with a green trash bag.

"Why are you limping?" Mr. Yee asked her. "You are young, you should be healed by now."

"I need my cast," said Lucasta, picking up her rabbit.

"Did you let your rabbit out of its cage?"

Benny asked her.

Lucasta frowned. "It hopped out when I went to put lettuce inside."

The shape in the sleeping bag groaned. It moved. Then it sat up.

Everybody could see that it was Roger Walski inside the sleeping bag.

"What's going on here?" he asked, rubbing his eyes.

"What are you doing on the ground?" asked Mr. Yee.

"I'm guarding my plot," Roger answered. "So that nothing else is stolen."

"Is that your breakfast in the big bag?" asked Benny, pointing to the bag.

"Bag?" asked Roger, looking around. "What bag?" Then he saw the big burlap bag sitting on the ground. "What's that? That wasn't there when I went to sleep," he said.

"That means somebody put the bag there after you fell asleep," said Henry.

"And that means you are not much of a guard," said Mr. Yee. "Not if somebody can sneak up in the middle of the night and deposit a big bag next to your head."

Roger scowled. "Never you mind," he said to Mr. Yee. He crawled out of his sleeping bag. As Roger crawled out of the bag, a clipboard and pen fell out of the bag. Henry stooped to pick them up, but Roger shouted at him. "No! Leave that alone!" Roger quickly grabbled the clipboard and pen and shoved them far into the sleeping bag.

Henry wondered why Roger didn't want him to see the clipboard. *I wonder what's on it,* thought Henry.

And then Henry noticed a small tool kit alongside the sleeping bag. When Roger saw Henry looking at the tool kit, he shoved it into the sleeping bag, also.

Roger stood and stretched. Then he leaned down and cautiously opened the lumpy burlap bag. "Cucumbers!" he said in surprise. "The bag is full of cucumbers!" Roger removed a cucumber from the bag, inspected it, and bit into it. Everybody heard the loud, juicy crunch as he did so.

"Good," Roger declared, "but they

wouldn't win a blue ribbon."

Violet saw Lucasta's rabbit sniff at the cucumber. The rabbit tried to jump out of Lucasta's arms, but she held it close and didn't allow it to escape.

Rabbits must like cucumbers, thought Violet.

Mr. Yee and Benny both took cucumbers out of the bag and bit into them.

"This is good," said Benny.

"But not good enough for a blue ribbon," said Roger.

"How can you tell?" asked Jessie.

Roger held out the half-eaten cucumber and pointed to its green skin. "The skin is too thick," he said. "A thinner skin is better because it's less bitter."

"That is correct," said Mr. Yee as he finished eating his cucumber. "This is a good tasting cucumber, but not quite good enough for first prize in a contest."

"Well," said Roger as he took several cucumbers out of the bag, "I'm going to take some of these home to eat. Everybody else is welcome to take some, too."

"Thank you," said Jessie. "We'll take some home to Mrs. McGregor."

"And I will take some, also," said Mr. Yee as he reached into the bag.

"What about you, Lucasta?" asked Roger. "Do you want the rest of these cucumbers for your rabbits?"

Lucasta stroked her Rex rabbit and shook her head. "No," she replied.

Roger Walski looked surprised. "No?" he asked. "Why not?"

"My rabbits are prize-winning rabbits," said Lucasta. "They deserve only prize-winning vegetables. They need to eat the very best in order to have the shiniest fur and brightest eyes."

Mr. Yee nodded his head slowly. "That is why you raised beautiful vegetables in your garden but did not enter them in the fair — you fed them to your rabbits instead."

"My rabbits are going to win first prize again this year," said Lucasta. "They win every year. That's important."

Lucasta turned and hobbled away, heading toward the barn across the road.

"I don't understand why her leg seems to be hurting," said Mr. Yee, looking puzzled. "Yesterday she had her cast off. Her leg should be healed by now."

Just then Henry remembered that he never got a chance to give Roger yesterday's message from Alex Kirk.

"Roger," said Henry, "Alex asked me to give you a message. He said, 'My father still says no.'"

"Is that so?" said Roger with a scowl. He bent down and rummaged in his sleeping bag. Finally he pulled out the clipboard and pen and held them to his chest. "We'll see about that," he said.

The children and Mr. Yee watched as Roger Walski walked away from them. They watched him walk up to Section B and talk to a gardener.

CHAPTER 7

# *Move the Gardens?*

After Roger departed, the children and Mr. Yee went to work.

Now that Jessie and Violet had done all the thinning, Mr. Yee showed them how to use a hoe to kill weeds.

"Oh," said Jessie, "this is so much easier than being on the ground and weeding."

"Yes," said Mr. Yee, "but don't hoe for too long, or you will get blisters on your hands. Start out for fifteen minutes today, then you can switch to something else, like carrying water buckets."

"I like to carry water buckets," said Benny, who was squatting down one row away. He was checking each strawberry plant to make certain it wasn't too dry, and to see which berries were ripe for picking.

As his sisters and brother helped Mr. Yee do the things that needed to be done in the garden, Henry started to repair the tomato stakes that the vandal had smashed.

*Hmmm*, thought Henry. The stakes were damaged, but they weren't damaged that badly.

Henry thought for a while, then decided he could pound two thin but strong stakes into the ground alongside the big stake. After he did that, he attached the big stake to the thin stakes, using a strong wire. Then he went to find Mr. Yee.

"What do you think?" Henry asked Mr. Yee.

Mr. Yee clapped his hands in excitement. "Excellent!" he said. "This is a wonderful way to solve the problem, because it leaves the old tomato stakes in place."

Mr. Yee reached out and touched one of the green tomatoes hanging from the first plant that Henry had worked to prop up. "You have done an excellent job, Henry, because you have thought of a way to keep the old stake in place. That means the tomato plant is not disturbed at all. And that means it is a happy plant and will produce wonderful tomatoes!"

"I'm glad you think this is a good idea," Henry replied. "I'll work on repairing the rest of the tomato stakes now."

"Good," said Mr. Yee. "You and Jessie and Violet and Benny are wonderful helpers."

Henry looked out across the garden, down toward the other sections. He could see Roger walking around with his clipboard, talking to gardeners.

"Ahh, yes," said Mr. Yee, following Henry's gaze. "You are curious about what Roger is up to."

"Yes," said Henry. "I am."

"And so am I," said Mr. Yee. "When you finish the tomato stakes, why don't all five

of us take a break and walk to the other sections."

Henry smiled. "That's a very good idea. We can talk to the other gardeners."

And so, after Henry finished with the tomato stakes and Jessie and Violet finished hoeing and watering, and Benny finished checking and picking the strawberries, the children and Mr. Yee felt they had accomplished a lot.

They put the garden tools away, into the community tool shed, and they washed their faces and hands at the water spigot. Then they walked toward Sections B, C, D, and E, and talked to the other gardeners.

Right away, in Section B, they learned that Roger Walski had been trying to get others to sign a petition. The petition asked the Greenfield Town Hall to relocate the community gardens to another area next year — because the gardens here were being vandalized.

"But we don't want to move to another area," said a gardener in Section C. "We like it here, where Mr. Kirk has built beautiful storage sheds and put in water spigots."

"That's right," said another gardener. "We like it here. We just want somebody to find out who's knocking down our tomato towers and breaking our trellises."

"And riding a three-wheeler over our lettuce and kale and chard!" said a third gardener angrily.

"We're going to help find who's doing

this," Henry said to the gardeners.

Jessie and Violet and Benny nodded. Mr. Yee nodded, also.

Then the gardeners went back to their gardens, and the Aldens and Mr. Yee saw Mrs. McGregor coming to pick them up.

* * *

That afternoon Grandfather was back home from visiting his sister, Aunt Jane. And when he heard what his grandchildren had been doing, he called his old friend Mr. Yee and invited him to dinner.

Everyone was very happy as they sat down to another one of Mrs. McGregor's wonderful meals. This one was full of garden-fresh vegetables that the children had brought home with them.

Mrs. McGregor brought a cucumber salad to the table. "My goodness," she said, "I've never seen so many cucumbers in my life! Who picked all these cucumbers at once, and why?"

Benny told her how that morning they had

found two lumpy sacks at one of the gardens. One sack held Roger Walski, the other held many, many cucumbers.

"Roger Walski?" asked Grandfather. "I know him. He owns and runs the big construction company that built the new Greenfield Town Hall."

"It is a beautiful town hall," said Mr. Yee as he gently scratched the place where his cast met his hand.

Henry spoke. "I wonder what Mr. Kirk was saying no to, in his message to Roger."

"I don't know," answered Mr. Yee, carefully accepting more cucumber salad, using his left hand to spoon it onto his plate.

"Several years ago, Roger wanted to buy the Kirk farm," said Grandfather. "But I haven't heard anything about that in maybe three years."

"Maybe Roger wants to buy the farm again but Mr. Kirk still won't sell," said Jessie.

"Mr. Kirk would never sell his farm as long as he can use it to grow crops," said Mr. Yee. "He loves to farm."

"Would he sell the part that the community garden is on?" asked Henry.

Mr. Yee shook his head. "Not as long as somebody wanted to garden on it. Mr. Kirk loves to see people grow food and eat it."

"Alex is like his father," said Benny. "Alex likes to grow food for people to eat."

Mrs. McGregor brought more food to the table: barley and mushrooms, sauteed chard, and carrots sauteed with ginger and orange juice.

"Look," said Violet as the carrots were being served. "Aren't the purple carrots beautiful?" she asked. "I love how they're purple on the outside and orange on the inside." She turned to Mr. Yee. "Why did you decide to grow purple carrots instead of the regular orange ones?" she asked.

"I grow orange carrots, too, Violet," said Mr. Yee. "But I like the purple ones better. I think they taste better, and purple vegetables are very healthful."

"Getting back to Roger Walski," said Grandfather, "I heard he wants Greenfield to build a new health center, with a pool, several running tracks, and a weight room."

"Taylor would like that," said Jessie. "She loves to exercise." Jessie told Grandfather who Taylor was.

"Roger is petitioning the other gardeners," Henry said. "He wants them to agree to move the community gardens."

"But the other gardeners don't want to move," added Jessie.

"I don't want the gardens to be moved," said Benny. "I like them right where they are. And I like the rabbits, too," he added.

"Well," said Mr. Yee with a laugh. "you and I agree and disagree, Benny. I like the gardens where they are, but I don't like the rabbits."

Grandfather laughed, too. "Albert, I know you. What you really mean is that you don't like the rabbits on the loose, where they can trip people."

"Perhaps that is so," said Mr. Yee.

By the time dinner was finished, everybody was full. But not too full — they had each saved room for fresh strawberries.

After the berries were all gone, Grandfather and Mr. Yee went to sit on the porch and talk. The children stayed behind to clear the table for Mrs. McGregor.

"This was a very interesting dinner conversation," said Jessie as she collected the used bowls.

"Yes," said Henry as he stacked plates. "We learned something very useful."

"Was it about Mr. Walski?" asked Benny.

"Yes," said Henry. "We need to talk to Roger Walski tomorrow morning."

CHAPTER 8

# *The Vandal*

The next morning it was Grandfather, not Mrs. McGregor, who dropped Mr. Yee and Henry, Jessie, Violet, and Benny off at the community gardens. Grandfather then drove away and the five gardeners walked past Sections E, D, C, and B, saying hello to all the other gardeners.

And once again, as the children and Mr. Yee left these sections behind and walked toward Section A, they saw trouble.

Taylor Harris and Alex Kirk were standing

in front of Taylor's fenced-in garden, shouting at each other. A big American blue rabbit hopped past Alex and into Mr. Yee's garden.

"You're the one!" shouted Taylor. "You're the garden thief!"

"I am not!" shouted Alex. "You don't know what you're talking about!"

The children ran up to Taylor and Alex. Mr. Yee hurried into his garden, after the rabbit.

Just then Roger came out of his garden and walked up to Taylor and Alex.

"What's wrong?" Henry and Roger asked the question at the same time.

"Alex Kirk has been vandalizing our gardens — that's what's wrong," snapped Taylor.

Roger took a step backward. He looked confused.

"You don't know what you're talking about," Alex replied angrily. "I would never vandalize anything, especially a garden!"

"Then explain your footprints," said Taylor, pointing at the ground.

Everybody looked down at the grass they were standing on. It was dusted with a white powder. At first it was hard to notice that there was something on the grass, but after Taylor pointed downward, it became clear.

Jessie looked at the trail of whitish powder. It started at the outside of Alex's garden, went past Taylor's garden, past Mr. Yee's garden, and stopped at the end of Roger's garden.

And: there was one set of footprints in the powder. The footprints came from the direction of Lucasta's empty garden and stopped about halfway to Mr. Yee's garden. It was clear to Jessie that whoever had been walking there walked right into Mr. Yee's garden.

"I came here late last night," said Taylor, "and sprinkled some bonemeal fertilizer across the grass. I wanted to see who was walking around here breaking Mr. Yee's tomato towers." She folded her arms across her chest. "And now I've caught the vandal. Those footprints match Alex Kirk's shoes," she said, pointing down to Alex's feet.

Everybody could see that the footprints leading up to where Alex was standing were

the same as the footprints that walked down the row of gardens and turned into Mr. Yee's plot.

Taylor pointed to Alex's hands. "He has a hammer in his hand, to smash tomato towers with."

"I don't smash tomato towers!" Alex shouted. "I was coming to fix something."

Roger Walski rubbed his chin with a hand. He started to say something, then stopped.

Henry spoke up loudly, so that Taylor and Alex would stop shouting. "Alex isn't the vandal!" said Henry.

Taylor stopped shouting at Alex and turned toward Henry. "What do you mean?" she asked.

Henry looked at Roger. "Don't you have something to tell us?" he asked.

"What?" sputtered Roger. "Me?" He backed away another step. "No, I don't have anything to say. Except . . . except that I don't think Alex is a vandal."

"I'm not," said Alex.

"We think you do have something to tell us," Jessie said, looking at Roger.

"What?" asked Roger.

"We know you're trying to buy the land the community gardens are on," said Jessie. "We think you want the town of Greenfield to build an exercise center on this land."

"What?" said Taylor. "Build a gym on the community garden land?"

Mr. Yee came out of his garden and joined them. He was holding the big bluish-gray rabbit in his arms and feeding it leaves of lettuce.

"That is why you want people to sign your petition," said Mr. Yee, nodding his head. "You want to buy this land and then sell it to the town."

Alex spoke up. "That's right," he said. "Roger has been trying to buy this land from my father, but my father won't sell."

"What's wrong with a gym?" demanded Roger. "Exercise is good. Greenfield could use a nice new exercise center. And this land is so close to the center of town."

"But this land is our garden," said Taylor. "It's good, rich land, meant for growing food."

"That's right," said Alex.

"Are you the vandal?" demanded Taylor. "Did you break Mr. Yee's tomato posts? Did you run over everybody's kale and lettuce plants?"

Roger didn't say anything.

"You drive a three-wheel ATV," said Henry. "And yesterday you had a tool kit with you, with a hammer and saw. You were going to use it to break down more trellises and towers."

Roger looked sad. He stared at the ground. "I'm sorry," he said at last. "It was wrong to damage people's gardens. But I really want this land! I thought if gardeners left, Mr. Kirk would sell it to me."

"It doesn't matter how much you want this land" said Taylor, "it's very wrong to do what you did."

Roger looked ashamed. " I shouldn't have done it," he admitted. "I won't do it again."

"I think you should help the people whose gardens you vandalized," said Violet softly.

Roger looked at Violet. He sighed. "You're right," he said. "I have to apologize to each person I hurt. And I have to fix what I broke."

Roger turned to Mr. Yee. "Albert, I'm sorry I broke your tomato stakes. I'll put in new ones for you tomorrow."

Mr. Yee scowled. "That was very wrong of you, Roger. But I don't need your help because Henry has already fixed the tomato stakes." Mr. Yee stroked the rabbit and fed it more lettuce. "You go help the other people, Roger."

"And you owe everybody for all the vegetables you stole," said Taylor.

"But I didn't steal any vegetables!" shouted Roger. "I'm not a thief!"

Taylor looked at Roger. "Then Alex must be the thief," she said.

But when everybody turned to look at Alex, he was no longer there.

CHAPTER 9

# *Thinking It Through*

The footprints in the lime showed that Alex had walked away, back toward the Kirk farm.

"Hmmpph," said Taylor. "I'm going back to my garden, but I'll talk to Mr. Kirk later. Alex can't be allowed to steal our vegetables."

"I have to apologize to a lot of people," said Roger. "I'll get started."

The children and Mr. Yee watched Taylor unlock her garden gate, go into her garden, and lock the gate behind herself. Then they watched Roger walk to the far end of the community gardens, where he began to talk to a gardener.

Mr. Yee still held the big American blue rabbit.

"Is that your rabbit now?" Benny asked. He liked the way the rabbit's ears moved back and forth and how its nose twitched.

"No, Benny," said Mr. Yee. "It is probably Lucasta's rabbit. And I don't like rabbits." He fed the rabbit another lettuce leaf as he said this.

Henry and Jessie and Violet all smiled at one another.

"Come," said Mr. Yee. "We'll go to work."

Once they were inside the garden, Benny went straight to the strawberries and Henry went to the peas and beans.

Jessie and Violet went to the lettuce and carrots. Mr. Yee followed them.

"Oh, no!" cried Violet when they reached the rows of carrots. She pointed to the ground. "The garden thief has been here. He stole all the carrots!"

"What?!" shouted Mr. Yee. "My carrots! I always win a blue ribbon for my carrots!" He was very upset.

Jessie looked around. "Not all the carrots were stolen, Mr. Yee," she said. "Only some."

Mr. Yee and Violet looked where Jessie was pointing, and they saw that one long row of carrots had been stolen. But another long row was still growing, the feathery tops standing straight up.

"Ooohhh," said Violet. "The row of purple carrots is still here. So you can still win prizes for your purple carrots, Mr. Yee."

Mr. Yee handed the rabbit to Jessie. He stooped down and pulled out a carrot. It was long and straight, with a feathery green top.

Violet could smell the carrot the minute Mr. Yee pulled it out of the ground. "That smells so good," she said.

Mr. Yee snapped the carrot in half. Then he fed part of the carrot to the rabbit that Jessie was holding.

"We must find out who is stealing our vegetables," he told the girls. "It is a terrible thing to walk into your garden and find your vegetables missing. I think —" Mr. Yee stopped talking in the middle of his sentence. He pointed.

Jessie and Violet looked to where he was pointing. There, at the far end of the row that once held orange carrots, was a burlap bag. A lumpy burlap bag.

Without speaking, Mr. Yee and Jessie and Violet all walked toward the bag. Mr. Yee took the rabbit from Jessie and held it close. "You look," he told her.

Jessie knelt down and opened the bag. Inside were carrots: dozens and dozens of orange carrots. She took one out and handed it to Mr. Yee. "Is this one of your carrots?" she asked.

Mr. Yee shook his head. "No," he said. "I can tell by looking that those aren't my carrots. The variety I planted grow long and slender. The variety in the bag grows short and chunky. I do not understand," he said. "Somebody stole my carrots, and then that somebody gave me different carrots."

Benny and Henry came to see what was wrong, and Jessie told them about the carrots.

Henry picked up the bag of carrots and looked at the burlap bag itself, then at the carrots. “I think we have a lot of clues,” he said, “and we can talk about them at lunch, after we help Mr. Yee with his garden.”

“Good idea,” said Jessie. “I brought my notebook.”

And then the Aldens and Mr. Yee returned to garden work: weeding, thinning, tying up vines and climbing plants, and watering.

* * *

When it was time for lunch, Mr. Yee, still holding the rabbit, went off to see how Roger was doing with his apologies. The children found a shady spot under a big tree that grew nearby. They sat and opened the lunches that Mrs. McGregor had packed for them.

As they ate, they talked.

"I don't think that Roger is the thief," said Henry. "He thought that breaking things in people's gardens would make them want to move. I don't think he thought about stealing their vegetables."

Jessie and Benny and Violet agreed.

"Roger was very upset when his cucumbers were stolen," said Benny. "He was not cool."

The others laughed.

"No, Benny, he wasn't as cool as a cucumber," said Jessie.

"When it comes to the garden thief," said Henry, "some clues are more important than others."

"When it comes to the thief, the burlap bags aren't important," said Violet as she munched on one of the cucumbers that Mrs. McGregor had packed.

"I agree," said Jessie. "And when it comes to the thief, the footprints aren't important, either."

"Well," said Benny impatiently, "what is important when it comes to the thief?"

"Green trash bags are important," said Henry.

"Lucasta has a green trash bag," offered Benny. "We saw Henry put it away."

"That's right," said Jessie. She paused in the middle of eating her sandwich. "The cobbler's apron is equally important."

"We saw a cobbler's apron hanging in the barn," said Violet. "But Alex put it away as soon as we saw it."

"We saw the apron not long after we saw Taylor's leg weights," said Jessie thoughtfully.

"Her leg weights have pockets, and so does a cobbler's apron."

"Are there any more cucumbers?" asked Benny.

Jessie gave him one of hers. "Blue ribbons are also important," she said.

"Blue ribbons are important to Taylor," said Henry. "She's never won one."

"And to Lucasta," said Benny. "She wants every one of her rabbits to win a blue ribbon."

"So," said Jessie, counting on her fingers, "we have three important clues about the thefts: the green trash bags; the cobbler's apron; the blue ribbons; and —" She looked at her sister.

"The purple carrots," said Violet.

"But nobody stole the purple carrots," Benny argued. "How can they be a clue?"

"Because," said Henry, "sometimes what isn't stolen is as important a clue as what is stolen."

The children got up and brushed the grass and twigs off their shorts.

"I wish the burlap bags were a clue," said

Benny. " I really like the burlap bags!"

Jessie tousled Benny's hair. "Oh, the burlap bags are an important clue, Benny. They just aren't a clue to the thief."

"That's right," said Henry. "Where have we seen burlap bags recently?"

"In the Kirk barn," Benny. answered eagerly. "They were hanging on the walls near the rabbit hutches."

"Taylor was with us," said Jessie. "She saw them, too."

"The burlap bags are important," said Henry, "but what's inside them is even more important."

Jessie spoke. "It's time for another trip to the Kirk barn," she said.

CHAPTER 10

# *The Thief*

Just as the children finished lunch and their discussion, Mr. Yee arrived back at his garden, still holding the rabbit.

Taylor came out of her garden and locked the gate. "I'm going to the Kirk barn," she said, "to tell Alex he has to stop stealing our vegetables."

"We're going there, too," said Jessie, "to tell the thief to stop stealing."

Taylor looked at Jessie. "Hmmm," said Taylor. "I notice that you didn't say exactly what I said."

Jessie smiled. "I'm glad that you noticed," she said.

"Hmmm," said Taylor as they walked. "Hmmmm."

When the group arrived at the Kirk barn, they saw Alex and Lucasta inside. Alex was putting vegetable seeds into peat pots. Lucasta was feeding her rabbits.

Before anybody else could speak, Lucasta came running up to Mr. Yee.

"What are you doing with Braxton?" she demanded. "Braxton is my rabbit. Give him back!"

"He cannot be your rabbit," answered Mr. Yee. "You said your rabbits never escaped their pens. This rabbit was in my garden, eating my vegetables."

Lucasta frowned. "Which vegetables?" she asked.

"Lettuce," said Mr. Yee. "Braxton likes lettuce."

"And carrots," said Violet. "He ate a carrot."

"A purple carrot?" asked Lucasta. "Braxton ate a purple carrot?"

"Yes," said Mr. Yee. "Purple carrots are very nutritious."

"Purple is my least favorite color," said Lucasta. She looked at her rabbit. "If Braxton ate a purple carrot, I don't want to enter him in a contest. "She looked at Mr. Yee. "You seem to like Braxton."

"Yes, I do," admitted Mr. Yee.

"Well, then, you can have Braxton if you want to," said Lucasta. "I don't want a rabbit who eats purple carrots."

Lucasta turned away and went back to the other rabbits.

Mr. Yee and Taylor and Henry, Jessie, Violet and Benny just stood there. They couldn't believe what they had just heard.

"That is not nice," muttered Taylor, "giving away her rabbit like that."

Benny looked at Mr. Yee and Braxton. "I think that Braxton will be very happy with Mr. Yee," said Benny.

Taylor looked down at Benny. "You're very wise for one so young," she said.

"Thank you," said Benny.

Alex had stopped planting seeds into peat pots. He had listened to the conversation, and he had frowned when Lucasta gave away her rabbit. Now he spoke. "If you came about the rabbit, you can go now."

"No," said Henry, "we came to name the garden thief and put an end to the stealing."

"Look at this," said Lucasta loudly, taking

a Rex rabbit out of its cage and bringing it to the group. “Isn’t she lovely? Look at her gleaming fur and her bright eyes. She’s going to win grand prize.” Lucasta stroked her rabbit. “And my other rabbits will win blue ribbons and red ribbons and yellow ribbons. I’m going to win a lot of ribbons this year.”

“Be quiet, Lucasta,” said Alex.

“No,” said Lucasta. “I deserve to win the prizes because I raise the best-looking rabbits.”

“You are a thief,” said Jessie. “You’ve been stealing everyone’s best vegetables to feed your rabbits.”

“She’s the thief?” asked Taylor, quite surprised.

“I should have known,” said Mr. Yee.

“It’s Mr. Yee’s fault,” said Lucasta, pointing at him. “He made me break my leg and so I couldn’t garden this year. But I need the very best vegetables for my rabbits to win.” She glared at the group. “You should be happy that your vegetables will help my rabbits win.”

"Our vegetables belong to us," said Taylor angrily. "They aren't for you to take."

"Taylor is right," said Mr. Yee. "It is wrong to take what belongs to somebody else, something they have worked hard to grow."

Taylor turned to the Aldens. "I thought it was Alex," she said. "How did you figure it out?"

"We noticed that sometimes Lucasta wore a cast on her leg, and sometimes she didn't," explained Jessie. "And sometimes she walked fast and sometimes she walked very slow — especially when she had the green trash bag wrapped around her cast."

"Green trash bag?" asked Taylor.

"Yes," said Jessie. "See that apron on the wall?" She pointed toward the rabbit hutches. "It has a lot of pockets in it."

"I see," said Taylor, "but I still don't get it."

"Lucasta tied the bag around her cast. She stuffed the stolen vegetables into the pockets, then covered everything up with the green trash bag."

Violet looked at Taylor. "You helped us

figure this out."

"I did?" said Taylor, confused.

"Yes. The day you showed us how lead weights slipped into the small pockets of your leg weights," said Violet. "Later that day we saw the apron with the many pockets. And later still we figured out what Lucasta was doing."

"And that's not all," said Violet. "The color purple helped us. It's my favorite color," she added softly.

"Ahh," said Mr. Yee. "I am beginning to see what happened. The garden thief took all my orange carrots. But the thief didn't take the purple carrots."

"That's right," said Violet. "The thief hates purple."

"Stupid purple carrots," said Lucasta. "I would never feed them to my rabbits."

"I will feed them to my rabbit," said Mr. Yee, petting Braxton.

Henry spoke up. "There was one more clue," he said, "something that puzzled us at first. Somebody was giving vegetables back to the people whose vegetables had been stolen."

He turned to Alex. "That was you," he said. "You were giving people vegetables from your own garden. You gave Taylor kale. You gave Roger cucumbers. You gave Mr. Yee carrots. You were trying to replace everything that had been stolen."

Alex nodded. "You're right," he said. "I figured out what Lucasta was doing." He frowned at his sister. "I told her she had to stop, that it's wrong to steal. But she wouldn't listen." He looked at everybody in the group. "I'm sorry you didn't like my vegetables," he said.

Everybody shook their heads. "Oh, we did like your vegetables," said Taylor. "The kale was delicious! I gave some to many different people, and they all loved it."

"The cucumbers you gave Roger are delicious," said Benny. "We had them for dinner and we had them for lunch."

Alex looked happier than he had. "That's good," he said. "I'm glad you liked the food

I gave you. That's what food is for: to eat."

"It is time for us to leave," said Mr. Yee. He looked at Lucasta. "Do not steal any more vegetables from our gardens," he told her. "If vegetables are missing, we will know it was you."

"If vegetables are missing, we'll go straight to your mother and father and tell them what you're doing," said Taylor.

Lucasta pouted. "Okay, okay. I won't take any more of your vegetables. I was getting tired of dragging them around anyway," she said. "But if my rabbits don't win grand prize, it's all your fault!" She turned and marched away, back to her rabbit hutches.

* * *

"Some people will never admit they have done wrong," said Mr. Yee as he and the Aldens and Taylor walked back to their garden plots.

"That's true," said Taylor, "and that's sad. But now," she said, rubbing her hands together, "let's get back to gardening! The county fair is just two weeks away."

Taylor unlocked the gate to her garden and went inside, waving a goodbye to the children and Mr. Yee.

The children walked into Mr. Yee's garden with him.

"Thank you so much for how you have helped me," he told them. "I could not have continued my garden without your help."

"We like helping you," said Henry.

"And we're learning a lot," added Jessie.

"And the vegetables are delicious!" said Benny.

Mr. Yee laughed. "Well," he said, "my cast comes off tomorrow. Would you like to keep helping me even though my arm will no longer be in a cast?"

All four Aldens eagerly agreed to help.

"Can we come with you to the county fair?" asked Henry. "We'd like to see all the vegetables we're helping you grow."

"Of course," replied Mr. Yee. "We can all go together." He looked around his garden. "I might win a prize for my purple carrots," he said.

He looked at Violet and Jessie. "If my purple carrots win a blue ribbon, I'll give it to you. You're the ones who thinned and weeded and watered the carrots."

"I want a blue ribbon, too," Benny announced. "I want to win it for your delicious strawberries — if I don't eat them all up in two weeks!"

*Before they were the Boxcar Children, Henry, Jessie, Violet, and Benny Alden lived with their parents at Fair Meadow Farm.*

*Turn the page for a sneak peek*

CHAPTER ONE

# *Good Times*

Henry stood in the doorway of the barn and looked out over the farm.

"I can smell spring," he said.

His younger sister Jessie leaned her pitchfork against the barn wall and stood next to him. There had been a spring snow in the night, but she could see grass. The sun was warm.

Jessie raised her head and sniffed.

Henry laughed.

"You look like Betty," he said.

Betty was one of their two cows. There was Boots who was mostly black and sweet and silent. But it was Betty who always stretched her neck out and put her nose in the air before she mooed. Papa called Betty "talkative."

Jessie smiled.

"It is spring," she said. "And I have my spring list."

Jessie took a piece of paper and a small hammer out of her pocket. She nailed the list on the wall.

Henry read over her shoulder.

"One: Make barn hideaway."

There was no number two.

"That's it?" asked Henry, grinning.

Usually Jessie's lists were longer.

"I've just started," said Jessie.

"What is a barn hideaway?" he asked.

"I'll show you," said Jessie. "Come."

Henry followed her to the ladder that went up to a loft. They climbed up.

The room was swept clean. There were two benches. There was a table with a vase with no flowers. A small, round window looked out over the next farm.

"A barn hideaway," said Jessie.

"It is," said Henry.

"Violet and Benny will like it," said Jessie. "Violet can do her sewing and painting up here. We can read books to Benny."

"And Benny can fall out the door and down the ladder," said Henry with a small smile. "We'll have to build a gate for Benny."

Jessie nodded.

"But he'll love it," she said.

Jessie frowned.

"I need more things for my list," she said.

They heard the sound of Papa's old gray car in the driveway.

Jessie and Henry climbed down the ladder and watched Papa walk up to the barn, carrying a cloth sack of nails and some boards for the stalls.

"Almost done?" he asked them.

"Just have to carry water for the cows," said Jessie.

Papa stood next to them.

"What are you looking at?"

"Spring," said Jessie and Henry together.

Their papa laughed.

"You're hopeful," he said. "There will be another good snow storm before it is really spring. This is March!"

"Any news from town?" asked Jessie.

Papa sighed.

"Bad news. People losing their jobs and houses. Trying to find other places to make a living. Many people leaving. Hard times."

"You're lucky to have your job," said Henry. "And Mama's baking for the market. It doesn't look like hard times here."

"I'm afraid you'll see hard times soon, Henry," said his Papa.

"I don't want to see hard times," said Jessie.

"I don't want to, either," said Henry.

"No one does," said Papa. "We are lucky to have paying jobs, but it means more chores for you, though," said Papa. "Being the oldest."

"And me," said Jessie.

"And you," Papa said.

"Everyone works at our house," said Jessie.

And that was true. Violet, who was ten,

helped with the laundry and set and cleared the table at dinnertime. And Benny? Benny was just five and he made everyone smile.

"That's Benny's job," Mama had said, "to brighten our days."

The door to the house opened suddenly and Violet and little Benny ran out into the snow, followed by Mama.

Benny lay down in the snow, making a snow angel, and Violet started rolling spring snow for a snowman. Mama looked up at the barn and waved.

"Come play!" called Violet.

Papa touched Henry then Jessie.

"Go on," he said. "I'll finish here."

Henry and Jessie ran whooping down the hill, slipping and sliding in the snow.

"Watch out!" called Papa. "Mama has a snowball!"

Mama laughed.

"I do!"

In the paddock Betty stretched out her neck and mooed loudly.

"Moo," called Jessie.

"Moo," called Henry.

"Moo," said Benny, pointing at Betty.

Behind them, in the barn doorway, their Papa smiled.

* * *

It was nighttime. Henry was reading a book in bed, the lamplight falling across the pages.

"Henry?"

Jessie stood in his doorway.

Henry put the book down on the bedside table.

"What?"

"I'm worried about what Papa said. Hard times."

"Sometimes things happen we can't do anything about," said Henry.

"Maybe we have to find a way to do something," said Jessie. "I need a longer list, too," said Jessie. "I need something exciting to add to my list."

"Maybe something will happen that you can add to your list," Henry said.

"It's too peaceful here," said Jessie. "Every

day is like every other day."

As it turned out, something would happen. Something not at all peaceful. Something Jessie and Henry could never have imagined.

It would happen the very next day.

*For more exciting Boxcar Children Mysteries, check out these titles:*

***#1 THE BOXCAR CHILDREN***
***THE BOXCAR CHILDREN® MYSTERIES***

HC 978-0-8075-0851-0 • $15.99/$17.99 Canada
PB 978-0-8075-0852-7 • $5.99/$6.99 Canada

"One warm night four children stood in front of a bakery. No one knew them. No one knew where they had come from." So begins Gertrude Chandler Warner's beloved story about four orphans who run away and find shelter in an abandoned boxcar. There they manage to live all on their own, and at last, find love and security from an unexpected source.

**#2 SURPRISE ISLAND**
***THE BOXCAR CHILDREN® MYSTERIES***

HC 978-0-8075-7673-1 • $15.99/$17.99 Canada
PB 978-0-8075-7674-8 • $5.99/$6.99 Canada

The Boxcar Children have a home with their grandfather now—but their adventures are just beginning! Their first adventure is to spend the summer camping on their own private island. The island is full of surprises, including a kind stranger with a secret.

***#3 THE YELLOW HOUSE MYSTERY***
***THE BOXCAR CHILDREN® MYSTERIES***

HC 978-0-8075-9365-3 • $15.99/$17.99 Canada
PB 978-0-8075-9366-0 • $5.99/$6.99 Canada

Henry, Jessie, Violet, and Benny Alden discover that a mystery surrounds the rundown yellow house on Surprise Island. The children find a letter and other clues that lead them to the trail of a man who vanished from the house.

GERTRUDE CHANDLER WARNER discovered when she was teaching that many readers who like an exciting story could find no books that were both easy and fun to read. She decided to try to meet this need, and her first book, *The Boxcar Children*, quickly proved she had succeeded.

Miss Warner drew on her own experiences to write the mystery. As a child she spent hours watching trains go by on the tracks opposite her family home. She often dreamed about what it would be like to set up housekeeping in a caboose or freight car—the situation the Alden children find themselves in.

While the mystery element is central to each of Miss Warner's books, she never thought of them as strictly juvenile mysteries. She liked to stress the Aldens' independence and resourcefulness and their solid New England devotion to using up and making do. The Aldens go about most of their adventures with as little adult supervision as possible—something else that delights young readers.

Miss Warner lived in Putnam, Connecticut, until her death in 1979. During her lifetime, she received hundreds of letters from girls and boys telling her how much they liked her books.